THIS IS THE
BEAR
AND THE
PICNIC LUNCH

For Helen with love
S.H.

For Christle, Mimi, Ruth and Didi
H.C.

1993 Impression
Houghton Mifflin Edition, 1991

Printed in the U.S.A.
ISBN: 0-395-53888-2
J-FL-99876543

THIS IS THE
BEAR
AND THE
PICNIC LUNCH

WRITTEN BY

Sarah Hayes

ILLUSTRATED BY

Helen Craig

HOUGHTON MIFFLIN COMPANY BOSTON

Atlanta   Dallas   Geneva, Illinois   Palo Alto   Princeton   Toronto

This is the boy

who packed a lunch

of sandwiches, chips and
an apple to crunch

This is the bear
who guarded the box

while the boy went to find
his shoes and his socks.

This is the dog
who sneaked past the chair

toward the picnic lunch
and the brave guard bear.

This is the bear
with his eyes half closed
who did not notice
the dog's black nose.

This is the bear

who was sound asleep

when the dog took off with

a tremendous leap…

onto the table...

down to the floor...

and off to hide

behind the door...

and all that he left
of the picnic lunch
was an empty box and
an apple to crunch.

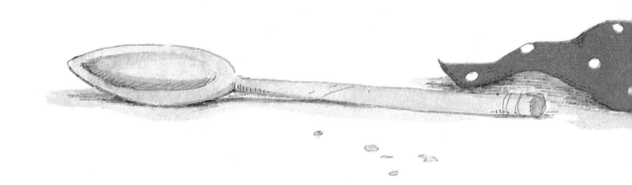

This is the boy
who looked everywhere

for his lunch and his dog
and his brave guard bear.

This is the boy

who heard the munch

of a dog and a bear

eating a lunch.

This is the boy
who tried to be angry

but decided instead

he was terribly hungry.

This is the boy
who packed a new lunch
of sandwiches, chips and
an apple to crunch.
And this is the bear who said,
"Haven't you guessed?
Picnics indoors are really
the best!"